LUCY & ANDY
NEANDERTHAL

Jeffrey Brown

CROWN BOOKS
for YOUNG READERS
New York

Thank you to my family, friends, publishers, and readers for all of their supports. Thanks also to Marc, Phoebe, and everyone at RH for making this book happen. And special thanks to Kevin Lee for giving me the nudge that led to the idea for this book.

For his expert assistance, grateful acknowledgement to Jonathan S. Mitchell, PhD, Evolutionary Biology, and member of the Geological Society of America, Society of Vertebrate Paleontology, and Society for the Study of Evolution.

All rights reserved. Published in the United States by Crown Books for Young Readers, an imprint of Random House Children's Books, a division of Penguin Random House LLC, New York.

Crown and the colophon are registered trademarks of Penguin Random House LLC.

Visit us on the Web! randomhousekids.com

Educators and librarians, for a variety of teaching tools, visit us at RHTeachersLibrarians.com

Library of Congress Cataloging-in-Publication Data is available upon request.
ISBN 978-0-385-38835-1 (trade) — ISBN 978-0-385-38837-5 (lib. bdg.) — ISBN 978-0-385-38836-8 (ebook)

Printed in the United States of America
10 9 8 7 6 5
First Edition

3

4

After a brief interruption, the hunter once again identifies his prey....

Silently, he creeps closer....

Waiting for the perfect moment, he prepares to pounce on his unsuspecting quarry....

MREEEEOWWRRRRR!

YEOWCH!

6

ACTUALLY, Neanderthals probably didn't have pet cats, because there were no house cats 40,000 years ago. The cats back then tended to be a lot bigger. Their pounces were much less friendly!

Cave lion →

European jaguar ↓

Nice kitties!

Ngandong tiger ↗

The saber-toothed cat Smilodon didn't live in the same places as Neanderthals, but the smaller Homotherium — scimitar cat — did. It wasn't as tiny as a house cat in reality, though. →

Mreow?

8

9

Mom, are Dad and Mr. Daryl back?

No, but that's why I was looking for you.

I think they'll be home pretty soon.

How do you know? Because they were going to the same area as last time, and you kept track of how long they've been gone?

No, I just have a feeling.

You're so weird, Lucy.

Why? It's not weird to figure things out.

You know, Margaret, I have feelings, too.

Scientists also thought Neanderthals only communicated by grunting. Now we know they could talk.

They were skilled hunters and cooked on fire hearths, just like early humans.

In fact, early humans and Neanderthals were alike enough that they even had kids together sometimes!

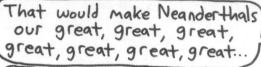

That would make Neanderthals our great, great, great, great, great, great, great...

You'll have to say "great" about 2,000 times.

LATER THAT DAY...

...great, great, great, great...

MUCH LATER THAT DAY...

...great, great, great, great-grandparents'!

Even if our research shows that the hairy, hunched-over, and dim-witted Neanderthal "caveman" is an inaccurate depiction...

We can still only imagine what life must have been like for them.

Look! Dad is out there!

I'm going to be the first to say hi to them!

Think again, slowpoke!

Must run faster!

Oops!

TRIP!

THUMP!

Thump!

Thump!

17

Apodemus sylvaticus (common name: wood mouse)

19

The Stone Age gets its name from the material used at that time for toolmaking: Stone, of course!

Flint

Basalt

Quartzite

Obsidian

Neanderthals created their tools using stones found nearby, but would also walk more than ten miles away to get better rocks that could be made into higher-quality tools.

My arms are sooooooooo tired....

And my legs!

We're going to make new tools out of these rocks.

Can we help, Mr. Daryl?

Yeah, can we?

Er....

Pleasssse?

Okay.

Now, where's Danny?

Follow me.

Here's the rest of the rocks, Mr. Daryl.

You know, there were already a ton of rocks right outside our cave.

But these are better... nice flaking, consistent feel, no cracks.

I'll go first—

You don't know what you're doing! Give me that.

Hey!

I'm glad you're both so eager to work, but we have to prepare the stones first.

Hey!

What? Do we have to wash them?

ptui!

Er, no, please don't spit on the stones.

shine shine

What we have to do is fire-treat them.

Bake rocks? Ha, good one, Lucy.

Lucy's right. We have to bury the stones under a fire, and afterward they'll be easier to work with.

Bury Bury

How long will this take?

Only a little while.

A LITTLE WHILE LATER...

Is it ready?

Not yet.

LATER THAN THAT...

Is it —

No.

STILL LATER...

Nope.

WAY, WAY LATER

Andy... ANDY! Wake up!

Zzzzz

The rocks are ready.

Huh? Oh, I was dreaming.

rub rub

Why are you looking at me like that?

I'm still dreaming.

You're definitely dreaming.

Are you dreaming, too?

Yes. I'm having a nightmare.

I'll show you how to do it, then you can all try.

I'm going to make the best tools!

I think you don't know what "best" means, Andy.

Okay, you need a rock, and a hard stone to use as a hammer.

After enough practice, you'll be able to tell just where to hit the rock...

CRACK!

...and knock off a nice, sharp flake.

Then you make some more flakes, using the whole rock...

A little more like this...

Crack!

Switch to a softer bone hammer for the finishing touches...

Crack! Tap!

crack!

Crack! Crack! Tap! Tap! Crack! Tap! crack!

There! A whole new set of cooking knives!

Very observant, Lucy. Do you think you can make more tools from one stone?

Hmmmm.

She knows she has to actually hit the stone at some point, right?

She's going to make it using her mind powers.

CRACK
CRACK
CRACK

There.

TWO hand axes.

Talk about wasteful! Look at all your extra pieces.

Yes, look at all these extra pieces. They'll make great spear points!

Ooh! Ooh! Let me try again!

Because you can't wait to smash your other thumb?

Crack Crack crack Crack crack Crack.

Ha! I made more tools than all of you combined!

That IS a lot of tools.

Yes. Very small tools.

These must be for itty bitty, teeny tiny spears.

I'm sure they're good for something.

Yeah, maybe Dad can use one to hunt those Apodemus sylvaticus.

How's the toolmaking going?

Good. The kids made some nice spear points.

ACHOO!

Hey!

Oops.

27

Wow, Phil, you've gotten much better. I'm pleasantly surprised!

Thanks, Mr. Charles.

Actually, I made those, Dad.

Really? Not bad, Lucy. Although...

These just need a little finishing.

Tap
Tap
Tap

Margaret made good spear points.

Ooh! I'll take those and start making new spears right now.

Dad, can I help?

Sure. Do you want to bring the stone tool you made?

Yeah, right here.

Where?

Here.

Uh, I don't see it.

It's right here. You can use it to hunt Apodemus sylvaticus!

!

By looking closely at Stone Age tools, scientists realized there were a few different types:

 Blade Your basic knife — as sharp as a surgeon's scalpel.

 Scraper Used to clean off animal skins.

 Hand Axe Good for heavy-duty cutting. No handle, but Neanderthals had very strong grips.

 Point Attached to a spear using pitch, a sticky tar.

Sometimes we find stone flakes that came from the same original rock. We can put them together to see how different tools were made step by step.

I think I'm missing a piece.

Luba, Andy will help me finish the spears so you can get Danny down for his nap.

Thanks, sweetie.

Do you want me to put the pitch on the spears? Or should I dip the spear tips in pitch? Or should—

Don't touch it! We have to handle the pitch just right or it won't work.

Which spear will I get to use on the hunt, Dad?

?

Andy, you're not ready for a mammoth hunt yet.

Yes, I am!

Andy, don't!

The pitch is still sticky!

Uh-oh!

Let me help. I've got it.

Okay, you can help now.

Wooden shaft →   Stone spear point   Covered with pitch, then tied with fiber

Pitch is hard to make, so Neanderthals must have been smart and skilled to be able to make it!

Mr. Charles? Mrs. Luba says there's lunch for you guys.

AAAHHH! What happened to you?!

Hi, Margaret.

If we held hands right now, we'd be stuck together forever!

You're making that face at me again.

Seriously, don't touch me.

Erf.

33

Oh, Andy, poor thing! You can't eat with your hands like that. Let's get you cleaned up.

Geez, Phil. You're eating a lot for someone who doesn't like acorns.

I don't, but I'm still hungry. Especially with all this talk about the mammoth hunt.

When will the mammoth hunt be, Dad? We'll plan tonight and hunt tomorrow.

We're going on the hunt tomorrow?

WE are. YOU'RE not.

35

You're still a kid. I'm not too young! My dad was younger when he went on his first hunt, right, Mom?

Well, yes, he was... So, can I go?

I guess maybe you're old enough....

YES!

Just ask Dad if it's okay.

Nooooo.

If he says no, you'll have to stay at the cave with Margaret.

YES!

I don't care how clean your hands are, you still can't touch me.

Nooooo.

I don't see why I can't go.

It's not safe.

kick!

The woolly mammoth lived in Europe and Asia until about 10,000 years ago.

Tusks could be as long as ten feet and may have been used to dig up tubers and roots

Ten feet tall — almost double the average Neanderthal's height

Small ears and lots of hair prevented heat loss in cold climate

Huge dung!

Mostly ate grass (possibly flattened by six tons of weight — that's as much as about a Tyrannosaurus rex!)

Phil, you're one of the hunters now. What do you think?

What about how we hunted the deer a few months ago?

We can herd them off a cliff. Splat!

Yah!

Rah!

uh oh!

We tried that once when I was young. It doesn't work as well with mammoths.

C'mon, up you go!

Go! Climb!

I'm not sure it can climb up there, guys.

38

You could push something ELSE off the cliff, though.

You could push rocks off the cliff and they land on the mammoths.

Seems simple, but you need rocks that are big enough, and the mammoth needs to be in just the right place at just the right time.

Ooh! Ooh! I know! We could build a trap!

That might work. What do you have in mind, Andy?

We dig a huge pit and fill it with spears.

Then cover it so it looks like grass.

And then we capture a baby mammoth and put it on the other side so the mammoths come to rescue it but fall into the pit instead!

We don't have time to set that up, but good idea, Andy.

pat pat

Why do you guys want to work so hard? Just wait for one to die.

That would be nicer to the poor mammoths.

Of course, we'd starve first.

So, the usual, then?

Yep. Chase one down and stab it until it stops moving.

We should scout the herd one last time and then get some rest.

Can I come?

It's not the hunt.

No, it's bedtime for you kids.

I don't know why Mom and Dad treat me like I'm a kid.

You ARE a kid.

Mom, why can't I at least watch the hunt?

You'll be able to.

Really?

Someday.

Please, Mom? I really want to go!

No, Andy.

Please please please please please?

Mom, tell Andy to be quiet.

Andy, go to sleep!

Pleeeeeasssse?

ANDY!

Yawn.

Andy, what are you doing?

Shhhh! I'm going to sneak along on the hunt. This is my camouflage.

Poor Andy. He really wants to go on this hunt.

Maybe your dad won't notice the walking, talking bush that's following them.

Margaret, I'm surprised you offered to stay behind and watch us and Danny. You said toddlers are stinky.

They are, but have you ever smelled a mammoth? Yuck!

45

46

Are you leading us to more berries? Margaret will like it if I bring her a wide variety of berry choices.

No, we're going to go watch the hunt.

What?! We'll get in trouble! Mom and Dad said we can't go.

We're not going **on** the hunt. We're just going to **watch** the hunt.

What about Margaret? She'll come looking for her snack.

Nah. Even if she didn't have to carry Danny, she's too lazy to chase after us.

Umm...okay.

But what if Dad sees us? He'll be angry...

Wait, get down!

Huh?

Why? Because of all the blood, and the stabbing, and the—

Ugh, stop talking or you're going to make me throw up again.

What are you doing?

Getting the berries for Margaret.

I bet these are her favorites. Do you think she'll start liking me?

Now I'M going to throw up.

What did you two do—go and plant berries, then wait for them to grow?

Berries!

I did pick your favorites, right?

Whatever. The berries are for your little brother. Where's my water?

Berries!

Uh...

You didn't try to hunt the water with that spear, did you?

Uh...

We're back!

Did you kids behave for Margaret?

Of course!

Just our normal, quiet, well-mannered selves!

Mama! Dada!

It was almost like they weren't even here.

Yeah, almost.

Heh heh.

Well, I hope your appetite is here. Look at all the mammoth we have for dinner!

60

Here you go, Dad.

Oh, thanks, Andy. We can use that later.

Phil already found some really good branches.

Mmm, that smells good.

Here's a steak for you, Lucy.

Can you take one to Mr. Daryl, too?

Here, Mr. Daryl— AAAAHHH!

What happened to your leg?!

Hm?

I hurt it on the hunt.

61

Oh, you mean this! It's a mammoth bone! Ha ha!

Oh, phew!

I'm just getting some marrow out. Do you want some?

Sure, thanks!

FATTY BONE MARROW!

An important source of nutrition for Neanderthals

Hyenas shattered bones, and other carnivores chewed off the ends to get at the plentiful deposit.

Neanderthals would split bone to extract as much tissue as possible.

Andy, did you eat all of your mammoth steak already? Do you want more?

Uh, no, no thanks. I'm... not hungry.

Stab chop stab

Gurgle

62

Like some modern-day human hunters, Neanderthals often held food with their teeth while cutting it. Scientists know this from tiny marks on Neanderthal teeth. The location and angle of the marks also show that most Neanderthals were right-handed!

Mom, do we have any more vegetables? Sorry, honey, that was all we gathered. There's lots of mammoth.

Stab stab chop

Ugh. Are you sure you aren't sick?

More!

I wish we could just call out to someone and they'd bring us the food we ordered.

And people think I have strange ideas.

Do you kids want to hear about the hunt now? No, that's okay, we saw —

Stab stab stab

We saw how much meat you brought back. How was the hunt?

OOF!

It started with ME. I had to confront the mammoth....

You have a long way to go before you have hunting skills like mine, Andy!

64

Are you getting emotional about missing the hunt, Andy, and having to sit around the boring cave all day?

Actually, we had an exciting day. Margaret sent us to look for berries.

Berries? Ooooh!

...but we ran into a CAVE LION! It chased us, but we were too fast.

Then there was a flood that almost washed us away and we had to make a tree bridge to escape!

And we narrowly missed being eaten by the cave lion on our way back to the cave.

Still brought the berries.

Really? That's amazing!

Why didn't you tell us sooner?

Wow!

No, not really. I made it all up.

Couldn't you tell?

Making up a story? What's the point of that? Everyone knows stories are about real stuff.

I'm telling you, there's the weirdest kids around here.

Ha. Nice throw. It WAS a nice throw. But a bad catch.

Bad catch? I asked you to HAND it to me!

Nice 'stache, Lucy.

Heh heh.

No, wait! Don't!

Being stuck inside all day won't be so bad with you two entertaining us.

Yes, carry on.

What are you drawing, Lucy?

71

Oh, is that a picture of Mom?

Mama?

What? No! It's a mammoth!

Oh, yeah.

Mamath?

That's pretty good. Can you draw some deer?

Yeah, cool. Now draw a... a cave hyena!

Draw me.

I can draw you, Margaret.

Dada!

That's good. Now draw a scimitar cat.

Yeah, draw Tiny.

No, draw a regular one.

Dada!

Deer.

Cave bear.

Another mammoth.

Me!

Here, Margaret, look!

That doesn't look like me at all!

Ha ha!

Dwaw?

Lucy? What are you doing way back here?

I just want to draw in peace.

That would look cooler if you colored it in.

Yeah...maybe if I had some of that color clay we saw.

By the river? You'd have to go out in the rain to get it.

Or YOU could get it for me.

No way. Puppy dog eyes won't work on me.

But I don't have your natural strength to carry it.

I AM pretty strong!

Thanks, Andy.

Why do I feel like I'm being tricked into doing this?

I got you every color I could find.

Can you mash them up? I need to think of what to draw....

This big, blank wall can be intimidating to an artist.

You could draw a story about me!

Oh, I know! I'll draw the mammoth hunt.

No, that's embarrassing! Draw a different story about me.

I'm not going to draw you throwing up, don't worry.

MREOWWR!

Tiny, that's not a real mammoth!

He's excited to see one his size.

Mew?

Hey, is that supposed to be Dad? Yeah.

Oh, that's Mr. Daryl. And Mom. Yep.

Who's that? That's just some dirt on the wall. Oh.

This is almost like art, Lucy. Like art? It IS art.

I guess it depends on what art is. What is art, then? You don't know anything about it.

Okay, I'll be back in a second. Where are you going? I'm going to bring everyone else to see. They'll know about art! Andy, don't—

I'm not ready for everyone to see my drawings. Andy? A second is over!

These are pretty amazing techniques, Lucy. Careful line-work to create a sense of depth, overlapping multiple figures for a feeling of dynamic movement.

You can see where the animal shapes have been carved into the wall before painting... it's so realistic you can almost feel the fur!

Of course, as her vibrant early style becomes more consistent, it also becomes stiff and overworked.

Not bad, Lucy. Although I'm not THAT old.

I think your other drawings were better. Now you're trying too hard.

What are you doing, Lucy?

Whatever. I could have drawn that.

smudge wipe wipe

Oh, yes. By erasing this priceless art, you attempt to question the value of creative expression in society.

Right. Like... getting rid of the drawings is the REAL art. Good thing you have me to explain your art...

Otherwise, it wouldn't make any sense.

I thought your drawings were wonderful, Lucy.

What gave you the idea to draw that? To celebrate the hunt? To pass on our knowledge? For good luck on future hunts?

No, I was just bored.

Hey! Where did everyone go?

Oh! It stopped raining. Wait up!

Ba ga ba bifftt!

What are you guys doing?

Andy was just telling us about how he outran a cave lion.

What? He didn't outrun—

Oh, you mean yesterday when everyone else was at the hunt! Right, yeah, totally outran a cave lion, yep.

If you could outrun a cave lion, you can outrun me, right?

Of course.

Okay. Ready...set...

Hm?

GO!

Eep!

Neanderthals may have used more energy for running than humans because they had shorter and thicker limbs.

GOTCHA!

WHUMP!

OOF!

That must've been a really slow cave lion.

It was, now that you mention it.

Yeah, it was... really old. And it couldn't see. And it only had, like, one leg.

Uh-huh.

I bet I could catch you with only one leg.

No way!

Catch me if you can!

Huff!

Wait a minute!

Huff huff!

86

Huff! Huff! Why - huff - aren't you - huff - chasing me?

Huff!

Got you.

Didn't even need <u>one</u> leg.

Wait, that was almost as if she gave me a half hug!

I suppose you outran the cave lion, too.

No, I just outran Andy.

Hey!

That's not hard. Not like outrunning a charging mammoth, like I had to!

Plus, I had to throw rocks at its head at the same time.

Big deal! Throwing rocks is easy!

Easy for me. See that pinecone?

I bet you I can hit it in one throw.

Like humans, Neanderthal shoulder joints allowed for good throwing movement.

Small stones perfect for throwing have been found with the remains of humans and Neanderthals.

Oops! Well, I can do it in two throws.

Er, three.

Four.

Five.

You meant that when you finally hit it, that's one throw?

Like you could do it.

I bet I can.

90

This place looks familiar.

Mom, I think you should take a look at Phil's head.

Oh, dear! Phil, what happened?

Bump!

Don't worry. I can't even feel it.

Dad and Mr. Daryl are getting more mammoth meat, so I'll go find some medicine. You kids'll have to keep an eye on Danny.

Ma!

Can't Margaret watch Danny?

I think she's going to be handling Phil.

Hi, birds!

Come back here!

Well, at least we'll be entertained.

Danny is not a toy, Andy.

pftt!

This is going to be boring.

My dad says only boring people get bored.

I'm still bored.

Exactly.

Exactly?

Here, Danny.

Don't give him that!

Why not? He likes it.

BAHH!

Let me have that, Danny. It's not for playing with.

Gah!

Next you'll want Danny to go on hunts, too.

No, I wouldn't. He has to wait until he's older than me.

Sti!

Have this small stick, Danny.

Whoa, this stick is so cool!

Careful!

That's too small! He could choke on it!

How about this one?

Too dirty.

Sti! sti!

This one?

Too sharp! He could poke an eye out.

Sti!

This one?

He's going to poke a lot of eyes out!

See? A stick would make him happy. You can't just give him what he wants whenever he cries.

WAHHHH!

Then what's the point of crying?

There is no point.

WANHHH!

I know how you feel. They took my stick away, too.

If we let Danny have a stick, he could clean up.

You're just spreading it around.

Sweep Sweep

Use some leaves!

FINE.

Not so many!

Leef!

WHUMP!

Ugh. Why do we always have to do things your way?

Danny, no, yucky!

POUNCE

Because I know what I'm doing.

You just think you know.

Oh, I'm Lucy, and I have so many ideas!

I can do ANYTHING in the world!

Snort

Not like my brother Andy who is so—

BRRRAAPPPP!

96

The largest and deadliest canine to ever live was the dire wolf. Fortunately for Neanderthals, dire wolves lived only in North and South America, while wolves in Europe were more like modern-day wolves.

Danny?

Danny!

We have to find him, or Mom and Dad will think I'm not ready for more responsibility.

Who's Danny?

You mean we have to find him before he gets HURT?!

That too.

We have to find him before your parents get back. If you get Me in trouble...

Eeek!

Don't worry, look!

What is that?!

It's a fake Danny. We can leave it here and no one will be suspicious while we're looking for Danny.

Creepy.

99

103

104

Do you feel better now, Phil?

Yeah, I think I do....

Do you feel like you're back to, uh... normal?

What do you mean?

You know, you used to be mean to me a lot, then you got hit in the head by a rock and started being nicer....

A rock? I don't remember that.

Yeah, Andy threw a rock and it hit you right in the —

Heh, let's not dwell on the past!

Andy threw...?

We're just glad you're feeling better!

Old buddy, old pal.

pat pat pat

114

Neanderthals didn't seem to use spices.
They didn't even have salt or pepper!

First clear
evidence of
cooking with
Spices: 6,000 years ago

Really, really
old mustard

117

Let's go see Mom. She'll know what to do.

Andy, it's your tooth, not your legs. We're not going to carry you.

Mom, my tooth—

Go talk to your dad, Andy, Danny just had an accident.

Dad, my tooth ith hurting tho bad!

Andy, I've told you before, you need to speak clearly or we can't understand you.

He can't talk, Dad. He has a bad toothache.

Andy, I've told you before, you have to take care of your teeth or—

Dad! Just help him.

120

Okay, okay. Let's take a look.

Thank th.

We just need you to stop moaning.

YIKES! You're right. We're going to have to pull that out.

I'll just reach in and—

OUCH!!

CHOMP!

Thorry.

Here, Andy, wrap this around your tooth.

I'm almost glad I followed along.

Oth-kay. Nowth what?

Avenge your finger, Dad.

Sweet! A tooth!

A sweet tooth?

It's not in very good shape, but it's probably not a sweet tooth. Neanderthals didn't have as much sugar and starch in their diets.

No soda? That's one reason their teeth had less decay and fewer cavities than humans today.

The first toothbrushes were small, soft twigs.

Some Neanderthal teeth have grooves from being scraped by small sticks — the first toothpicks!

What was all the wear and tear on Neanderthal teeth from?

They used their mouths to hold things. Their teeth seemed worn down from a lot of chewing.

They also didn't have dentists!

They didn't have doctors, either, but they did know how to use plants for medicine!

This tooth has tiny minerals on it from chamomile and yarrow.

Those plants don't taste good or provide much nutrition, but they have been used for medicinal purposes.

My mom made chamomile tea to help me feel better! I put lots of honey in it.

chamomile
(helpful)

Neanderthals must have had extensive knowledge of plants that they shared with each other.

After all, it's more effective to learn from someone else than from your own trial and error.

yarrow
(helpful)

Aloe
(helpful)

poison ivy
(NOT helpful)

Definitely! Just the thought of having to make my own aspirin gives me a headache!

127

Right, good thinking. Don't tell me, or else it won't be a secret anymore.

It's not a secret. We need you to go to the mammoth carcass and collect skins and bones.

Oh.

Since it's not a hunt, can I be in charge, Dad?

Ha ha!

No, Phil has a lot more experience. He'll be in charge.

But Phil is older, so he'll ALWAYS have more experience.

Keep working hard and maybe you can be my assistant someday.

We need to gather up tools to cut the mammoth hide.

Let me know when you're done.

Why does Dad like Phil so much?

Andy, you're picking up old, broken tool bits. You need to pick good ones.

Oh, now you want me to be YOUR assistant?!

I'm just trying to help you.

These are perfectly good.

Almost perfectly good.

This is probably enough.

CRUMBLE

Here you go, Phil.

NOW you show up. Just when I got comfortable. You were taking forever.

Why did you bring these? They're all chipped and worn down.

Our dad and Mr. Daryl took all the good ones.

Pftt. These are useless.

Toss!

Maybe not.

GRAB!

We can just refinish them.

There!

Tap
Tap
Tap
Tap

Good as new.

Flip

What?

CATCH!

Did you...make this...for ME?

No, I just made it, and you ended up with it.

Same thing.

Uh, no, it's not.

Thank you. I will treasure this.

Neanderthals were some of the world's first people to recycle!

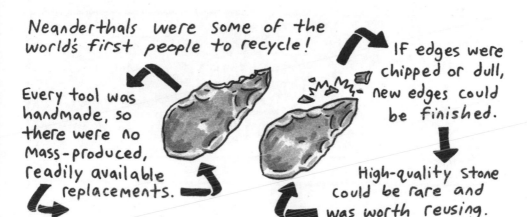

Every tool was handmade, so there were no mass-produced, readily available replacements.

If edges were chipped or dull, new edges could be finished.

High-quality stone could be rare and was worth reusing.

This is easier than making new tools.

Yours don't have the natural beauty of Margaret's, though.

Tap! Chip!

We don't have all day for your craft projects, Lucy. Let's go.

I don't want to hear any complaining. It's bad enough that I have to babysit you kids.

Isn't that complaining?

Yeah.

Museums use dermestid beetles to clean bones of flesh and organic matter, for easier study!

Even smallest bits are removed without damaging skeletons.

Doesn't clean off dirt or rock, though.

Also doesn't work on large animals like elephants.

Not bugs... probably Cave hyenas!

Cave hyenas? How do you know?

S'plorch

Ew.

I'm going to go clean my feet off.

What's that noise?

CREEEEAKkkk

What noise? I don't hear —

CREEEEEE CRACKK!!

—anythinnnnnngg!!

Go ahead. Say it. Say what?

Rub rub

You know. I wasn't going to say anything.

Just say it.

...

Oh, okay— Told you so.

You can put that bone with the stuff we're bringing back. Now cut some skins while I stand guard.

We can BOTH stand guard while the girls gather up the skins.

So you get to stand guard just because you're a boy? Well...

I'm the only one standing guard. Both of you two can get the skins.

What about Margaret?

I'm supervising.

Yeah. She's supervising.

Yeah.

Make sure you get the tusks. Those are cool.

Hmph.

I'll get them for you, Margaret.

Hmmm. Do some mammoths only have one tusk?

Of course not.

Then where's the other tusk? I'm telling you, something strange is going on.

The only strange thing is how you keep forgetting about the cave hyenas messing with stuff.

AROOOOOOOOOOOOOOO

Or wolves!

All right, let's pick everything up and head home.

141

145

Margaret makes the most boring clothes! She has no sense of style!

Well...

Sorry, Lucy, you're not ready just yet. But you can help Margaret.

Now you know how I feel!

No, because I'm actually good at making clothes.

You don't know that I'm not good at hunting, because I never get to do it!

Surrrrre.

So, if you're in charge, does that mean you'll stand guard while Phil supervises, and me and Andy do all the work?

Ha! Of course not. Have you seen the clothes Phil has tried to make?

Hey!

I can make clothes. It's easy. All too easy. I like a real challenge.

That's why I'm so good at stuff. I'm always challenging myself. You all can take care of the clothes.

He's probably going to challenge himself to take a really long nap.

He doesn't have to help? That's not fair.

Trust me, you don't want him helping with this.

At least we don't have to do all the work this time.

Actually, I'm going to be supervising.

Lucy, do what you need to do. Or whatever.

Pans.

Can my job be as your personal assistant, Margaret?

Uh, sure.

What would you like me to do first? Should we have a meeting to plan a schedule? Can I get you something? A snack? Or tools? Or —

Uhh...

You just do what Lucy tells you to do.

I'm going to supervise from somewhere else. Don't break anything.

Pans.

Here. Start chewing.

Chewing?

Everyone gets to tell me what to do.

Start chewing, Danny.

Ickth, chewy.

chew chew

Chew

chew chew chew

chew chew

Chewing on animal skins softened them, making them easier to work on.

Neanderthal teeth have marks showing they chewed on skins.

Not as good as chewing gum!

What are you guys doing?

Chewing the hides, of course.

But you don't have to slobber so much. Gross. And you didn't finish cleaning the skins off.

Gee, good thing you're back to help us.

I only came back because your mom saw me out there.

Mama?

So you're here to supervise now?

No, I'm here so it looks like I'm working hard.

If you know so much, show us how to prepare the skins.

We already used the scraper.

Scrapers can damage the skin. No wonder your mom didn't leave you in charge.

Go get me a deer rib.

This? No, that's a leg bone.

This? That's a back bone.
This? Hip bone.
This.

Are you messing with me?

Me? No, never! This?

See? Take the rib bone, press down, and rub it along the skin.

Did...did you just invent a new tool?

The lissoir — a bone tool used to smooth animal hides →

Some scientists think Neanderthals invented it, or they copied it from humans. Or both groups invented it separately — early great minds think alike!

Strong, but flexible, so it wouldn't damage the material

Twisted plant fibers were used as string!

Doesn't naturally grow that way!

The fibers have been found in Neanderthal territory from a time before humans. This shows that Neanderthals didn't always copy them.

If it looks <u>ridiculous</u>, it <u>feels</u> ridiculous.

You're just BEING ridiculous.

Are you saying your brother doesn't look silly?

He ALWAYS looks silly.

Yeah, but I look even SILLIER because of this <u>stupid</u> outfit.

If you don't like how they turned out, Margaret, maybe you should've at least helped make them.

See? Your MOM knew you couldn't handle this.

What are you upset about, Lucy?

Mom put Margaret in charge of making clothes instead of me.

Lucy didn't listen to Margaret.

That's because she didn't take charge. She didn't even help!

I tried to, Mr. Charles, but Lucy didn't want my help unless SHE could be the boss.

That's not true! I did all the work.

YOU did all of it?

Lucy just bossed me around. Right, Margaret?

Uh!

Yep.

Lucy?

Wow, what nice new outfits!

Mama!

But where was Lucy going?

Er...

Ugh! Why do I even bother?

Nobody gets me. They don't even appreciate everything I do!

I probably do look stupid.

I think your outfit is actually pretty cool.

You don't have to say that just to make me feel better...

You do feel a bit warm, sweetie.

That's because I just ran all the way back here!

Why doesn't anyone ever listen to me?

I believe you, Lucy. When I was young, I heard stories about another kind of people that sometimes came into our territory.

That would explain the strange things we've found lately...

The missing meat, only one tusk, the throwing spear...

I know! I've been trying to tell you.

Are you sure it wasn't cave hyenas?

166

The overall differences between early humans and Neanderthals were more pronounced than differences between any two humans today.

However, any single characteristic of Neanderthals — such as their brow ridge, lack of chin, or stout, thick limbs — can be found on different humans individually.

Lucy was right! We saw a clan not too far away!

They are a little different. Skinny. And tall. But they were NOT in the trees.

Do you think they're just passing through?

It looked like they were setting up camp.

Then we should welcome them to the neighborhood.

When humans and Neanderthals encountered each other, they could have traded goods and ideas.

Maybe Neanderthals learned from humans how to make sewing needles out of bone splinters.

Or humans learned how to adapt to a new environment from Neanderthal clans that had lived in the same place for thousands of years.

The meetings might not have been peaceful. After all, humans and Neanderthals would've been competing for the same limited resources.

Some Neanderthal bones show evidence of damage from stone tools or weapons.

We don't know for sure what happened, so we keep looking for more clues....

Are you excited about today?

Yes!

No.

Bounce!

Mom, should I put my old clothes on?

I'm not sure these can even be called "clothes" anymore, Andy. Why would you want to wear them?

I'm not used to these.

Maybe he doesn't want to look silly in front of strangers.

I think the new clothes look very nice. Didn't one of the other people say she liked them, Lucy?

Yes.

We should wear the new clothes. It might make the other people more comfortable. Too bad we don't all have new outfits!

We _do_ all have new outfits. We made them for everybody!

Oh, we didn't see.

I thought nobody liked the new clothes, so I put them away.

Can we try them on?

Okay.

Lucy, these are lovely.

Very comfortable!

They're great!

Whatever.

I think we're ready! Should we go?

Yes!

No.

Do you think we should've shaved?

Hm. Good question.

174

Humans have a hyoid bone — a small bone allowing the mouth and tongue to create complex sounds.

Scientists have discovered Neanderthals had a similar hyoid bone.

Neanderthals may not have been able to make the same range of sounds as humans, but they communicated with more than simple grunts and pointing!

Again? Yeah, well —

Shhh! Dad, I'm sure "again" means something different where they're from. Oh, okay.

I recognize you! We met in the forest.

Um, yeah, hi.

I'm Lucy.

Sorry if we scared you.

It's okay. I wasn't scared, I was, um... startled.

Cool!

Danny is my little brother. This is my other brother, Andy.

And there's Phil and Margaret.

Did you make your own outfit, too?

Humans migrated north from Africa, through the Middle East, spreading out as their populations grew.

There were no cars or bikes — people didn't even ride horses yet. So it took thousands of years!

Panel 1: What made you decide to move so far?

ZZZsnk+HM?
ELBOW!

Panel 2: There were more and more people around, so good hunting was getting harder.

Panel 3: We knew there were lots of animals around here, including mammoths. Those make great meals!

Panel 4: You've hunted mammoth already? Not exactly. We found a dead one.

Panel 5: Ohhh, wait. Was that a mammoth you guys had hunted? Yeah.

Panel 6: Sorry! Couldn't pass up a free meal, you know! I'm sorry!

Let us make it up to you. Have dinner with us!

Oh, okay. Thanks!

You can come back to our camp to eat. We've hunted a few different animals already.

Thank you!

We have lots of leftovers right now.

ANCIENT NEANDERTHAL DINNER MENU!

RED DEER
Was not artificially colored.

REINDEER
No evidence of ability to fly during holidays.

WILD HORSES
Saddles had not been invented yet.

AUROCH
Huge ancestor of modern cattle!

WOOLLY RHINO
Much furrier than you see in zoos.

EUROPEAN BISON
Used to roam where the Neanderthals called home.

Kids, we've been invited to dinner with our new neighbors!

It's the least we can do since we ate some of the mammoth they hunted.

Whoa, you hunt mammoth?

Yeah, all the time.

Really?

Wow!

I mean, not me personally.

Yet.

Oh. Huh. Yeah.

C'mon, Lucy, we'll show you our camp!

I didn't find any suitable place on my search.

Maybe our new friends can help. This is Charles.

What are you looking for?

A good place to live....

You're not just passing through? It's a lot warmer where we're from. We don't want to get caught in the real cold.

Where do you all live? We live in a cave not far from here.

You live in a cave? Cool! Can we live there, too?

Where is it?

Yeah, we could all live there together!

Uh, well, maybe?

Give her some space! You don't have to let us live with you, Lucy.

Oh, but it's okay. It'd be fun if you lived with us, Claire!

Thanks, Lucy. Maybe we can come for a visit first!

Hey, something just peed on my head!

What is it?

It's snow!

Snow?

You're with me?

Yeah.

We don't need a bunch of extra people in our cave.

You're WITH me!

It's bad enough I have to share a cave with you.

Still. You're with me.

Is this normal?

It is for this time of year.

It doesn't get colder than this, does it?

Well...

Brrrrrrr

Don't worry. Your camp will be enough shelter for now, and this snow will melt fast.

That's good to know!

Mommmmmmm! Can we go home now? It's cold.

Okay. Go ask your sister if she's ready to go.

Home!

C'mon, Lucy. Mom says it's time to go.

Already?

Thanks for having us for dinner, Claire. Maybe you can come over to our cave for dinner next time?

You better catch up with your brother, Lucy!

Okay. Bye, Sasha!

...I found ONE good cave.

Hm?

It's occupied, though.

I thought so.

There's more of us. We can take it over, I'm sure.

Yes!

RRRRRRR

191

This is the MOST exciting thing that has ever happened EVER!!

Dad, can the kids come over to play, do you think?

Sure.

I don't want them coming over. I think they're up to something.

Up to something? Then why would Chris let me have one of his spears?

Fwish! Fwish!

Margaret doesn't want them coming to our cave, either. Right, Margaret?

True.

Margaret doesn't want you there, either, Andy.

Also true.

I think they're really nice, Andy. You just need to get to know them!

Peepul!

Meeting new people could be great for us, Andy. With a bigger group, it'll be easier to hunt!

Yeah, and now I'll never get to go.

Maybe we'll have more babysitting help, too.

I wonder if they can show us how to make some new tools.

I wonder if they'll kick us out of our own cave.

I can't wait for tomorrow, Mom!

Time for bed, Andy.

Mreow?

You won't like them, either, Tiny.

What if they eat cats for breakfast?!

THE END

...OF THE NEANDERTHALS?!

Some of the first Neanderthal fossils were found in Germany in 1856.

Workers digging in a limestone quarry

At first, scientists were unsure what (or rather, who) those bones were from....

It's a new ancient species of humans!

Nonsense, it's just the bones of someone with a vitamin deficiency.

It is ancient, but it's not the ancestor of humans.

← OLD-TIMEY SCIENTIST GUYS →

Eventually, more bones were found and identified as Neanderthal: a species of people that died out as early humans spread across the world.

By excavating the floors of caves, we can see how generations of Neanderthals used the same caves again and again.

Over thousands of years!

Stone tool fragments (40,000 years old)

Ash from hearths (50,000 years old)

Mammoth bones (70,000 years old)

In fact, sometimes Neanderthals didn't get to eat much of anything and went hungry. We can tell by studying microscopic growth rings on their teeth, which show major life events.

I don't see any growth rings.

That's because you're not a microscope!

Dairy cows that provide milk didn't exist at the time, so Neanderthals got milk by nursing from their mothers.

Growth rings added every day

The growth rings show when Neanderthal children stopped nursing— a little earlier than humans.

That also may mean that the mothers weren't just at home caring for the children.

It may make sense to think Neanderthals behaved the same way as humans from a few hundred years ago, and that women took care of the children.

Scientists can't assume that, though. The bones of both male and female Neanderthals are similar in size and strength.

Which means that over their lifetimes, both genders did similar kinds of work.

We've found only a few complete skeletons, along with just hundreds of other Neanderthal bones. The female bones show the same wear and tear as the male bones.

Male and female Neanderthals apparently died at the same ages in equal numbers, so neither gender lived a more dangerous life than the other.

Neanderthals lived in small close-knit groups, or clans, occupying relatively small territories.

Early humans seemed to live in larger groups, with more extensive social networks covering larger areas.

By today's standards, their social networks were tiny!

Beep!

Tap
Tap
Tap

So the differences between them weren't just physical, like how human shoulders have a slightly wider range of throwing motion than Neanderthals.

But some differences didn't make much of a difference, like the larger noses Neanderthals tended to have.

Didn't scientists think the large nose could help breathing in a cold environment?

Now we think it didn't help much. There's no indication Neanderthals had a better sense of smell, either.

Humans may have had an advantage in sense of smell – through wolves that could track prey by scent. Wolves and humans could have helped each other hunt more successfully.

And defend against other predators. That would definitely have given humans an edge over Neanderthals, but they didn't have pet wolves, did they?!

The earliest signs of wolves being tamed are from about 40,000 years ago, just when early humans appeared in Neanderthal territory.

Wolves may have begun living closer to humans to scavenge campsites, over time becoming more and more comfortable with people.

Humans may have raised orphaned wolf pups, which became domesticated dogs many generations later.

I'm glad training my dog didn't take thousands of years!

A theory is an explanation of some aspect of the world, based on facts that have been confirmed by experiment and observation. Discovery of new evidence can lead to new explanations.

The stone tools that were found a hundred years ago still look the same as when they were found — it's how we understand them that has changed.

Science isn't set in stone!

Understanding the past is part of understanding who we are.

Learning about how Neanderthals lived helps us see why we live the way we do now.

And that can help us figure out the future — how we can live the best lives possible!

Right now your best life is going to be helping me organize all of these artifacts!

Some paleontologists work at museums. These are just a few museums you can visit to learn more about Neanderthals and early humans!

THE FIELD MUSEUM
Chicago, USA

Also has a great collection of dinosaur fossils - including Sue the T. rex!

Not actual size

NEANDERTHAL MUSEUM
Mettmann, Germany

Located at the site where the first Neanderthal fossils were found and covers the evolution of humankind.

AMERICAN MUSEUM OF NATURAL HISTORY
New York City, USA

Check out the Hall of Human Origins!

A NEANDERTHAL TIMELINE*

*Dates subject to change, as new discoveries are made.

2.5 million years ago: First stone tools are invented.

NEW!

1.8 million years ago: First Neanderthal ancestors leave Africa.

He's running away from home.

800,000 years ago: First fire hearths begin to be used.*

Ow! Ow!

* Also 800,000 years ago: First fingers burnt while cooking.

500,000 or more years ago: Ancient Neanderthals begin to evolve.

You look different.

500,000 years ago: First shelters are constructed.

400,000 years ago: Hafted tools, wooden spears, and pigments are made.

How do I look?

Great!

180,000 years ago: Neanderthals become a distinct species.

170,000 years ago: The earliest clothes are made.

40,000 to 50,000 years ago: Early humans arrive in Neanderthal territory.

30,000 to 40,000 years ago: Neanderthals become extinct.

FACT VS. FICTION

While most of Lucy and Andy's story is based on the best of our knowledge about Neanderthals, there are some parts that might be stretching the truth....

DID NEANDERTHALS HAVE PET CATS? No, unfortunately not. Cats weren't pets until about 5,000 years ago. But cats are fun to draw and make funny characters!

DID NEANDERTHALS LIVE IN SUCH SMALL CLANS? Yes, but maybe not quite as small as Lucy and Andy's clan. Neanderthals probably lived in groups of 10 to 15, while early humans lived in groups of 25 to 30.

DID SOME NEANDERTHALS GET BAD ROCKS FOR TOOLMAKING? Yes, sometimes tool debris from poor-quality stones is found near debris from good stones. Neanderthals who were just learning probably practiced on the stones of lesser quality.

DID NEANDERTHALS EAT ACORNS? Remains found at cooking sites indicate that they did. Humans have a long history of eating acorns, and you can still eat them today, with the right recipe!

DID NEANDERTHAL WOMEN HUNT? Almost certainly. Scientists still debate whether men hunted more, but Neanderthal women at least participated in some, if not all, hunting.

DID NEANDERTHALS HAVE GOOD FASHION SENSE? Neanderthals didn't have time to worry about style, and their clothes were simple and useful, although they may have decorated them with pigment.

COULD NEANDERTHALS AND HUMANS TALK TO EACH OTHER? They didn't have the same language, but that wouldn't stop them from communicating. After all, people from different countries today still find ways to communicate with each other, even without knowing each other's words.

A BRIEF MESSAGE FROM THE AUTHOR OF THIS BOOK

ME

Hi.

A few years ago, I had the idea of drawing a book about "cavemen."

Living in Chicago, I love going to the Field Museum and looking at the Ice Age skeletons....

And I've always been fascinated by ancient cave paintings!

After seeing BBC shows like <u>Walking with Dinosaurs</u> and <u>Walking with Cavemen</u>, I knew I wanted my book to be based on the latest science.

Humans did NOT live with dinosaurs, Fred Flintstone!

Before I could start drawing, I had to dig through a lot of books. Almost a hundred!

It's interesting to see how our view of Neanderthals has changed over the years.

Of course, since new information is always being gathered, our view of Neanderthals has even changed while I've been writing this book!

Another new discovery!

Now I have to redraw this page that I already rewrote?!

Someday this book may be outdated, too, but with the help of scientists, I've tried to make it as accurate as possible.

But since this book is a made-up story, I still get to use my imagination!

Accurate? That doesn't even look like me.

Giggle!

Thanks for reading!

A BRIEF HISTORY OF CAVEMEN IN BOOKS & MOVIES

Alley Oop (1932)

Comic strip caveman traveled through time

Tor (1953)

Adventure comic book took place one million years ago

B.C. (1958)

↑ Newspaper comic strip chronicles the lives of a group of cavemen and women

Flintstones (1960)

Cartoon about prehistoric family paralleling the modern world

Captain Caveman (1977)

Super-powered caveman can pull objects from his hair

Clan of the Cave Bear (1980)

↑ Historically researched novel later became a movie

Quest For Fire (1981)

Movie shows early humans trying to control fire 80,000 years ago

↓

Caveman (1981)

Comedic film shows Ringo Starr as caveman named Atouk

←

Unfrozen Caveman Lawyer (1991)

Television comedy sketch about caveman who becomes a lawyer

↓

Encino Man (1992)

Caveman frozen in ice thaws out in this comedy film

↓

The Far Side (1982)

Newspaper comic often featured goofy cavemen characters

↓

GEICO Cavemen (2004)

→

Television commercials humorously depict two cavemen frustrated at being thought of as stupid

The Croods (2013)

Animated comedy film shows cavemen surviving in fantastic imaginary world

↘

Margaret, would you go outside and check on Lucy and Andy? I'm worried, because it's freezing out there.

I could stay here with Danny while you go check on them.

I would, but Danny has a cold....

sniff sniff

On second thought, I'd be happy to go.

I just need to put my winter clothes on.

TWO HOURS LATER

Hm?

Oth, hith, Marthret!

Andy, what are you —? Never mind. Where's your sister?

Dowth there.

Cath you help me? My thung ith thuck.

Are they okay?

By their standards, everything is perfectly normal.

Margaret is right. You _are_ strange.

Heh.

Winter continues in Lucy & Andy Book 2! Coming soon!

Jeffrey Brown is the author of numerous
bestselling Star Wars books, including
Darth Vader and Son and the middle-grade
Jedi Academy series. He is not as old
as ancient fossils yet, but he does
have 2.2% Neanderthal DNA. He lives
in Chicago with his wife and sons,
who are not actually allowed to draw
on the walls. Most of the time.

jeffreybrowncomics.com
P.O. Box 120, Deerfield, IL 60015-0120, USA